T0198395

Hi My Name is Fear

Conscious Kids

Zainab Ansari

Archway Publishing books may be ordered through booksellers or by contacting:

Archway Publishing
1663 Liberty Drive
Bloomington, IN 47403
www.archwaypublishing.com
844-669-3957

ISBN: 978-1-6657-0986-6 (sc)
ISBN: 978-1-6657-0987-3 (e)

Print information available on the last page.

Archway Publishing rev. date: 08/02/2021

Hi my name is fear! F.E.A.R
False - Evidence - Appearing - Real

All human actions are motivated at their deepest levels by either me (fear) or my opposite, love.

In truth there are only two of us, (fear and love) we are the opposite ends of the great polarity. We are the two points, the Alpha and the Omega which allow the system of relativity to exist.

I like to creep into your thoughts and manipulate your decisions, regardless of what your intentions are.

I stay hidden behind every idea and thought you ever have, persuading you in every way to change your mind.

I don't care if you are about to do something great, brave, generous, inspiring, or heroic, I am always standing on the sidelines persuading you to quit or change your mind.

I create thoughts of failure, loss, and inferiority.

Every decision you ever make arises out of one of two possibilities; me or love.

"I am the energy that contracts, closes down,
draws in, runs, hides, hoards, harms.

Love is the energy which expands, opens up,
sends out, stays, reveals, shares, heals.

I cling to and clutch onto all that you have,
love gives all that you have away.

I hold you close, love holds you dear.

I grasp onto you, love lets you go.

I wrankle, love soothes.

I attack, love amends." (Neale Donald Walsh,
Conversations with God Book 1)

I am born from an illusion called death, but death is not real. Therefore I am not real.

Death actually means life, and is simply a shift in perspective. There are two perspectives of life. The Microcosm and The Macrocosm.

In the Microcosm you are living as a human being. In the Macrocosm (after you "die"), you are living as a soul. In the Microcosm you are living with time and space, in the Macrocosm there is no time and space.

All that happens when you die is your thoughts create your reality instantaneously. When you are alive your thoughts create your reality within time. This is just a shift between one perspective to another. Because time slows us down in our human form, we forget that we are actually creating our reality with our thoughts. We think things are happening to us rather than us making things happen. This brings us to creating our reality either through our uncontrolled thoughts, or collective consciousness (the consciousness of people on earth). If we understand that we are creating our reality with our thoughts, we would change our lives forever. This is exactly what happens when we die, when we shift to the Macro perspective. We travel with the speed of thought in a dimension of no time and space. The secret to life is to come to this realization before we die.

Physical | Metaphysical

Life is eternal. You are life. Life can never die, just as energy can never die. It can only be transferred. Once you "die" you will have the same choice you have now, create your reality through your own thoughts (except instantly because there is no time, also allowing you to be in more place than one, including being with your loved ones on earth), create your reality through uncontrolled thoughts (which won't last very long because you will realize instantly that you are creating with every thought, - instantly in no time / space, or create your reality through collected consciousness, which is the other souls. You will also either decide to stay as a soul only, or choose to cause yourself to forget this all over again by going back to human form (usually a new one, because you've finished the experience you chose to have in the previous one), and start all over again! Because the joy is in the experience of realizing this exact truth all over again! When you "die" you "know" the truth. When you live, you can experience what you know after you die!

However, dying is not the only way to leave your body (time / space dimension), you can achieve this through meditation as well. Meditation is controlling your thoughts by not thinking at all for a period of time in which you create a space in which the soul is isolated and becomes separate from the body. This is also a timeless space. Same rules apply.

Now, how would you live your life if you understood that death was just a shift in perspective of your current life??? Think of it as your life right now except with magical powers! ;)

So don't ever be afraid, because you can never die.

Energy healing technique for expelling fear out of
your body; (Donna Eden; Energy Medicine)

Hold your right hand in front of you with the palm of your hand
facing down, take your first two fingers on your left hand and begin
tapping in between your ring finger and pinky finger about an inch
after where your hand begins (on the outside of your hand). Keep
tapping it. If the fear still persists, switch to the opposite hand
and in the same spot begin tapping repeatedly. This will remove
the fear from your body. Everything is energy, we are energy.

Written By
Zainab Ansari

Printed in the United States
by Baker & Taylor Publisher Services